Successories®

Great Littl
The Peak Perfo man

By

Brian Tracy

CAREER PRESS
3 Tice Road, P.O. Box 687
Franklin Lakes, NJ 07417
1-800-CAREER-1; 201-848-0310 (NJ and outside U.S.)
FAX: 201-848-1727

SUCCESSORIES®: GREAT LITTLE BOOK FOR THE PEAK PERFORMANCE WOMAN
ISBN 1-56414-331-7, $6.99 / Cover design by Jenmar Graphics
Typesetting by Eileen Munson
Printed in the U.S.A. by Book-mart Press

To order this title by mail, please include price as noted above, $2.50 handling per order, and $1.50 for each book ordered. Send to: Career Press, Inc., 3 Tice Road, P.O. Box 687, Franklin Lakes, NJ 07417. Or call toll-free 1-800-CAREER-1 (NJ and Canada: 201-848-0310) to order using VISA or MasterCard, or for further information on books from Career Press.

Library of Congress Catalog Card Number: 97-75077

Never sell yourself short. Anything anyone else has done, you can probably do as well.

The only real limits on your potential are the limits you set on yourself.

Women-owned businesses employ more people than the entire Fortune 500 combined.

Women are forming new businesses at double the rate of men, and succeeding at three times the rate.

Women are the most powerful influence group in America at almost every level.

Women determine or influence 80 percent of the buying decisions in the U.S. economy.

More women are graduating from more universities and colleges with higher degrees than ever before in human history.

Women are rising to positions of leadership in virtually every field in America, and the rate is accelerating.

Peak performance begins with your taking complete responsibility for your life and everything that happens to you.

Always look to yourself as the primary creative force in your own life.

"No one can make you feel inferior without your consent."
—Eleanor Roosevelt

Remember always that you are a thoroughly good person, possessed of enormous potentials you have not yet tapped.

Accept that you are where you are and what you are because of your own choices and decisions.

Refuse to make excuses or blame anyone for anything.

Set clear goals and make written plans for each part of your life.

Goal-centered living leads to the activation of your full capacities.

What do you really, really want in life? What can you do today to begin achieving it?

Be selfish—make your own happiness the central organizing principle of your life.

Your aim should be to fulfill your potential and become everything you are capable of becoming.

What would you dare to dream if you knew you could not fail?

Set peace of mind as your major goal and organize your life around it.

Refuse to compromise what you know to be right for anyone or anything.

"To achieve something that you have never achieved before, you must become someone you have never been before."
—Les Brown, motivational speaker

Always live consistent with the very best that is in you, the very best that you know.

Identify your unique talents and abilities and then put your whole heart into developing them to the maximum.

Develop a clear vision for yourself and your life for the future.

Measure your progress continually. Is what you are doing right now moving you toward your life goals?

Set clear goals for personal and professional development.

Your most valuable asset in the marketplace is your earning ability. Do something to increase it every day.

Imagine your ideal future. Visualize yourself as if your life were perfect in every respect.

The starting point for making better decisions is for you to stop making *worse* decisions.

Love is by far the most important thing of all.

The greatest treasures of your life are associated with the people you love and who love you in return.

The greatest joys of life are happy memories. Your job is to create as many of them as possible.

Always give without remembering and always receive without forgetting.

Your name is the most important sound in your world. Give it with pride.

Identify the major obstacle that stands between you and your goal and begin today to remove it.

What one skill, if you developed it, could have the greatest positive impact on your career? This is the key to your future.

Think on paper—write and rewrite your major goals every day.

Practice creative abandonment with activities that are no longer as important to you as other things have become.

Your ability to set priorities on your time and your life will determine your happiness as much as any other factor.

What activities give you your greatest sense of joy and happiness in life?

In your work, always ask, "What are my highest value-added activities?" Work on them exclusively.

Your ability to write goals and create written plans for their accomplishment is the *Master Skill* of success.

Always work from a list. Write it out, organize it, and work on your most important task.

Continuous learning is the minimum requirement for success in your field.

Invest continually in personal growth and self-renewal.

Take excellent care of your physical health. Energy and vitality are essential to success and happiness.

Be clear about your goals. Be flexible about the process of achieving them.

Goals are dreams with deadlines. Set a time line for your goals.

There are no unrealistic goals; only unrealistic deadlines.

"To be all that you can be, you must dream of being more. To achieve the possible, you must attempt the impossible."
—Karen Ravn, writer

Optimism is the one quality more associated with success and happiness than any other.

Every situation can be a positive situation if you look upon it as an opportunity for growth and self-improvement.

Look for the good in every person and every situation. You'll almost always find it.

When God wants to send you a gift, He wraps it up in a problem. The bigger the problem, the bigger the gift.

You develop courage by acting courageously whenever you feel like acting otherwise.

"The key to success is to determine your goal and then act as if it were impossible to fail—and it shall be!"
—Dorothea Brande, American writer

Turn every experience into a learning experience. Seek the valuable lesson in every setback or disappointment.

Your self-esteem is the key measure of how well you are doing as a human being.

The more you like yourself, the better you do—and the better you do, the more you like yourself.

Control your inner dialogue. Talk to yourself *positively* all the time.

Become an unshakable optimist. Say, "I like myself! I like myself! I like myself!" over and over.

Begin each day by saying, "I believe something wonderful is going to happen to me today!" And it will.

Keep yourself positive by saying, "I believe in the perfect outcome of every situation in my life."

Refuse to criticize, condemn, or complain. Instead, think and talk only about the things you really want.

Your outer world of experience will always be a reflection of your inner world of thought and feeling.

You become what you think about most of the time. So think about what you want, and not about what you don't want.

You inevitably attract into your life people and circumstances in harmony with your dominant thoughts. What are they?

How you feel on a minute-to-minute basis is the true measure of how well you are doing. And you are in charge.

Resolve to be a master of change rather than a victim of change.

No one *makes* you feel anything. It is how you react and respond that determines your emotions.

You deserve the very best life has to offer. Reach out for it.

Once you have set a clear goal for yourself, resolve to persist until you succeed.

Whatever you believe, with feeling, eventually materializes in your reality.

Your self-limiting beliefs hold you back more than anything else. And most of them are untrue.

Your self-image determines your level of performance and effectiveness. What is yours?

All improvement in your life begins with an improvement in your mental pictures.

Flood your mind continually with pictures of the health, happiness, and prosperity that you desire.

Career success begins when you determine exactly what it is you are ideally suited to do.

Your emotions are determined 95 percent by how you talk to yourself. Continually repeat, "I feel happy! I feel healthy! I feel terrific!"

What skills or abilities have been most responsible for your success in life to date?

If you won $1million cash today, and you could work at any job, what job or field would you choose?

Dream big dreams! Imagine that you have no limitations and then decide what's right before you decide what's possible.

What one goal, if you achieved it, would have the greatest positive impact on your life?

What sort of activity has always been easy for you, but difficult for most others?

Start with the end in mind. Describe your ideal job, career, and work environment.

What steps could you take right now to begin turning your dreams into realities?

Perhaps the most important word in success and happiness is the word, "*ask.*"

Ask for what you want. Ask for help, ask for input, ask for advice and ideas—but never be afraid to ask.

Ask politely. Ask expectantly. Ask positively. Ask warmly. Ask sincerely. Ask curiously. Remember, the future belongs to the *askers*.

Ask for the job you want. Ask for the salary you want. Ask for the responsibilities you want.

The more specific you are about the job you want, the easier you are to hire.

Take complete control of your career path by research, planning, and active career development strategies.

When interviewing for a job, go prepared with a list of questions for the interviewer.

Do your homework—research the company and industry before the interview.

Network continually—85 percent of all jobs are filled through contacts and personal references.

Send a thank-you note after every interview. It will often tilt the balance in your favor.

Offer to work for a month at no pay to demonstrate your talents and your value to the company you wish to work for.

Work all the time you work! Develop the reputation for being the hardest-working person in your firm.

A reputation for hard work will bring you to the attention of key decision-makers faster than anything else you can do.

The formula for success at work is simple: Start a little earlier, work a little harder, stay a little later.

Become computer-literate and then computer-fluent. If you're not networking, you will be *not*-working.

School is never out for the Peak Performance Woman. Learn something new each day.

Read one hour in your chosen field every single day. This translates into one book per week, 50 books per year.

Take all the training you can get. Aggressively seek out new seminars and courses that can help you.

Turn your car into a learning machine—a university on wheels—by listening to audio programs while you drive.

Focus continually on performance and results—get the job done fast.

Manage your time well. Make every minute count.

Prepare for every meeting. Everyone is watching, especially your boss.

Those who do not speak up at meetings are considered by others to have nothing to contribute.

Volunteer for additional work and continually demand more responsibilities.

If all you do is all you're doing, all you'll get is all you're *getting*.

Your success in life will be in direct proportion to what you do after you do what you are expected to do.

If you never do more than you are paid for, you will never be paid for more than you are doing today.

Take advantage of your employer. Take every opportunity to expand your skills and abilities.

If you applied for your current job today, would you get it? Why? Why not?

What is your next job going to be? Job change is inevitable, but salary increases are not.

The market only pays excellent rewards for excellent performance, average rewards for average performance.

Pay any price, make any sacrifice, overcome any obstacle—but become one of the very best people in your field.

It doesn't matter where you're coming from. All that matters is where you're going.

You can learn anything you need to learn to achieve any goal you can set for yourself.

Your life only gets better when you get better, and you can improve without limit!

Good enough seldom is. Set excellence as your standard and refuse to compromise.

The future belongs to the competent. Never stop striving to be better.

You will always be paid in direct proportion to the work you do, how well you do it, and the difficulty of replacing you.

The only real security you can ever have is the ability to do a job uncommonly well.

Whatever job you take on, make yourself valuable, then indispensable.

Go the extra mile in your job. There are never any traffic jams on the extra mile.

Whatever your job title, you are in the business of customer satisfaction. Who is your customer?

Your customer is anyone who depends on you, or who you depend upon for success.

Your boss is your primary customer. What does he or she need to be satisfied?

The greatest *demotivator* in work is not knowing what's expected. Be sure you do.

Always work on your boss's top-priority tasks. What are they?

The very worst use of time is to do very well what need not be done at all.

Taking the time to do an excellent job at a low-priority task can sabotage your career.

What can you, and only you, do that, if done extremely well, will make a real difference to your company?

Your ability to set priorities and then get the job done fast will put you onto the fast track of your career.

The greater the impact of your work on customers and cash flow, the more important you become to your company.

Knowledge is power. Specialized knowledge or skills in your field enhance your promotability.

Superior performance is the key to high self-esteem and recognition.

Specialization and excellent performance are essential to advancement in your career.

Ask your boss for advice on how to get ahead in your career. Then, take it!

Dress for success—95 percent of the first impression you make on others is determined by your clothes.

Birds of a feather flock together. People like to promote people who dress the way they do.

Dress for the job you *want*, not the job you have.

Dress the way the top women in your industry dress, in every respect.

Speed is the currency of the 90s and beyond. Move fast when opportunities present themselves.

Thank the people who help you. Express appreciation on every occasion.

Dress professionally—create an image of strength and competence.

Be loyal to your boss, your company, your co-workers. Someone is always listening.

You develop power in your career by becoming a valuable resource to your boss and your company.

The better you get at what you do, the more power and influence you have.

The more people like and respect you, the more open they are to your influence and persuasion.

The more you help and support others, the more power and influence you will gain.

Never use your sex as an excuse for poor performance.

If you have a problem with someone you work with, discuss it with that person in private.

Your success in your career will be directly related to the number of people who know you and respect you in your field.

The more you like and respect yourself, the more you will like and respect others and the more successful you will be.

Leadership is the willingness to accept responsibility for results.

Your ability to get along well with others will determine your happiness and success as much as any other factor.

"Self-discipline is the ability to make yourself do what you should do, when you should do it, whether you feel like it or not."
—Elbert Hubbard, writer and speaker

Courage is your willingness to take action with no guarantee of results.

Integrity is the most desired, demanded, and respected quality of leadership.

See yourself as self-employed—act as if you owned the place.

Always be preparing yourself for a new, higher-paid job with greater responsibilities.

Develop a sense of urgency. Fast tempo is essential to your success.

People who get the job done fast are considered to be better and more competent.

Your ability to make decisions and take action is essential to putting your career onto the fast track.

Leadership is the ability to get followers. The more you support others, the more they will support you.

Develop a mentor at each stage of your career—someone who will give you guidance and advice.

Control your emotions. Take a deep breath and count to 10 before reacting.

The person who asks questions has control. Use questions to control the conversation.

Never assume you understand. Ask the questions.

If your job is customer satisfaction, your real job title is *Problem-Solver*.

Your ability to solve problems effectively determines how high you rise in your career.

Be creative. Always seek for faster, newer, better, more efficient ways to resolve the problem or get the job done.

Get the facts. Ask questions and listen intently to the answers before responding.

Resist pressure for immediate decisions. Ask for time to think the situation through.

Fast decisions involving people are almost invariably wrong decisions; take your time.

Learn to negotiate well on your own behalf—for your salary, increases, promotions, and responsibilities.

Preparation is the mark of the professional. Do your homework before the negotiations.

Never accept a job or a salary the first time it is offered. Ask for time to think it over.

In negotiating your salary, always ask for more than you expect to get.

Be specific. Be clear about exactly what you have to do to get an increase.

Be prepared to walk away from any situation that is unacceptable to you. This is the ultimate negotiating tool.

Timing is an essential element in negotiation. Pick your time and place with care.

Allow time for mental digestion. When you propose a new idea, give the person time to think about it.

Your success will be affected by the quality and quantity of new ideas you suggest.

You are a potential genius—the number of ideas you can suggest for improvement are virtually unlimited.

Your ability to achieve your own financial independence is vital to your self-esteem and self-respect.

You are only as free as your options and your well-developed alternatives.

"If you cannot save money, the seeds of greatness are not in you."
—W. Clement Stone,
American businessman and billionaire

You only feel happy to the degree to which you feel you are in control of your own life.

Think long-term. Plan and save today for a secure and independent life tomorrow.

Delay gratification. Resist the urge to spend everything you earn, plus a little bit more every month.

You are ultimately responsible for achieving and maintaining your own financial security.

Investigate carefully before you invest. Spend as much time researching the investment as you spend earning the money.

Money is hard to earn and easy to lose. Guard yours with care.

Make your own financial decisions. Never depend on anyone else.

Pay yourself first! Save 10 percent or more of your gross income every single paycheck.

Accumulate a minimum of three months' expenditures in a safe place—and never touch it.

The habit of regular saving plus the miracle of compound interest will make you rich.

Make your financial independence a primary goal in life and begin working toward it today.

Everything you have in your life you have attracted to yourself by being the person you are.

You can have, be, and do more because you can change the person you are.

You will always be paid in direct proportion to the value of your service to others.

If you want to earn more, you must first learn more.

Peak performance comes from a feeling of continuous growth and development in your personal value.

Commit to excellence! Resolve to become outstanding in a key job-related part of your life.

Treat yourself as a lifelong "do-it-to-yourself" project. Strive for feelings of inner harmony, balance, and peace of mind.

A positive mental attitude and peak performance comes from a positive response to stress.

Stress arises when you feel you are controlled by people and circumstances outside of yourself.

Get your time and your life under your own control to reduce stress and improve performance.

Positive, continuous action toward your goals is the very best antidote to worry.

Would you take your current job today if you had it to do over? If not, what are you going to do about it?

Make every minute count. The average person wastes 50 percent of her time in idle socializing and personal business.

You perform at your best when you are working continually on high-priority goals and objectives.

Choose your boss carefully! Your relationship with your boss is a key to peak performance.

Fire your boss! Never stay in a negative situation. Your life is too precious.

People don't change—in most cases, they become even more so.

Be flexible; be willing to consider the possibility that you could be wrong.

Don't be afraid to say, "I changed my mind!" when you get new information.

When you are with your family, be there 100 percent of the time.

Place your relationships at the top of your hierarchy of values and organize your entire life around them.

It's *quantity* of time at home that counts, and *quality* of time at work. Don't mix them up.

Spend uninterrupted chunks of time with the most important people in your life.

How do children spell LOVE? T-I-M-E!

The value of a relationship is in direct proportion to the time that you invest in the relationship.

Your relationships can be made to increase in value by your investing more time in them.

Women are complex and subtle. Men are simple and direct.

Accept complete responsibility both for under-standing and for being understood.

Men have sight; women have insight. You are very perceptive.

Denying or refusing to deal with some unpleasant fact in your life is the source of most stress and unhappiness.

Whenever you are unhappy for any reason, ask yourself, "What is it in my life that I'm not facing?"

You are where you are and what you are because of all your previous choices and decisions.

To improve your life, be prepared to make new choices and decisions.

Stress comes from within—it is your reaction to circumstances, not the circumstances themselves.

You are never upset for the reason you think you are; it is always something else.

When dealing with negative people, remember that you are not the target, just the victim.

Take time each day to sit quietly by yourself to relax, meditate, pray, and listen to the silence.

Get so busy working toward something that is important to you that you have no time to suffer stress, tension, and worry.

Time management is really life management. Peak performing women use their time well.

Concentrate on the few major areas where superior performance will bring outstanding results.

Think before you begin. Prior planning prevents poor performance.

The value of anything can be determined by how much of your time and life you are willing to trade for it.

Make a list. People who work from a written list are 25 percent more productive than those who don't.

Plan every week the Sunday before. Plan every day the night before.

Eliminate low-value time-consumers. Reduce and restrict television watching, newspaper reading and telephone socializing.

Keep your telephone calls brief—get on and off fast.

Practice single-handling with every task. Once you begin, stay at it until it is complete.

Take a speed reading course. Learn how to get through more material faster and with greater retention.

Analyze what your time is worth and value your activities accordingly.

There is never enough time to do everything, but there is always enough time to do the most important things.

What is the most valuable use of your time, right now?

Get your life in balance. What should you be doing more of? Less of?

Describe your ideal lifestyle; what could you do today to begin creating it?

Plan and schedule time with your family and friends in advance, just as you do with business commitments.

Reserve and pay for your family vacations at the beginning of each year. This guarantees that you will go on them.

Follow your personal energy cycle. Do important tasks when you are most energetic and alert.

Network continually with other successful, positive men and women.

Get up one hour earlier and use the time to think and plan your day in advance.

Do laundry as it comes up rather than saving it for a particular day.

Do grocery shopping only once per week, at one store. Use a list and shop during off hours.

Prepare and stockpile multiple amounts of a cooked dish for thawing and eating later.

Bunch your tasks. Do several identical tasks together to save time.

Spend time alone with each child each day. At bedtime is ideal.

Foster independence among your children. Encourage them to cook, clean, and contribute.

Combine your errands—do several in one trip.

Select an easy-care, wash-and-wear hairstyle.

Lay your clothes out the night before.

Each person has far more weaknesses than strengths.

The peak performance woman concentrates on performance, not politics.

Avoid stereotypes. Both men and women are combinations of strengths and weaknesses.

The purpose of an organization is to maximize individual strengths and make weaknesses irrelevant.

Take yourself seriously at work. Dress in such a way that others take you seriously as well.

"The best direction to ride a horse is the direction it is going."
—Mary Baker Follett,
1920s management consultant

Set high standards. See yourself as a role model for others.

Superior women carry themselves as though everyone were watching even when no one is watching.

You must often work harder than the men around you and appear superior to them to be accorded the same respect and treatment that they receive.

Leave your personal problems at home. Don't share them around the office.

Be direct in your speech. Don't beat around the bush when trying to make a point.

Speak up when you disagree. Silence is often interpreted as agreement, ignorance, or stupidity.

Put your whole heart into your work. Don't hold back.

"Never, never cry or become emotional at work. It can only hurt you."
—Diane Feinstein, U.S. Senator

Develop resilience and bounce back. Resolve to bounce instead of break when you experience setbacks.

Develop a compulsion to closure. Stay at one job until it is complete.

Accept feedback and self-correct. Learn from every experience.

Your body is the temple of your soul. Treat it lovingly and with care.

Peak Performance Women don't necessarily make the right decisions. But they make their decisions right.

Be more concerned about what's right rather than who's right.

Work harmoniously with others. Be pleasant, positive, and agreeable.

Practice the Golden Rule in all your interactions. Treat others as you would like to be treated.

Be willing to take risks and move out of your comfort zone in the direction of your dreams.

You do not need to be other than you are. You only need to be all of what you already are.

"Courage is rightly considered the foremost of the virtues, for upon it, all others depend."
—Winston Churchill

Every great move forward in your life begins with a leap of faith, a step into the unknown.

Continuous personal and professional development is the springboard to peak performance.

Nothing great is ever accomplished without persistence.

About the author

Brian Tracy is a world authority on time management and personal performance. He teaches his key ideas, methods, and techniques on peak performance to more than 100,000 people every year, showing them how to double and triple their productivity and get their lives into balance at the same time. This book contains some of the best concepts ever discovered.

Other best-selling audio/video programs by Brian Tracy

- *Action Strategies for Personal Achievement*
  (24 audios / workbook)

- *Universal Laws of Success & Achievement*
  (8 audios / workbook)

- *Psychology of Achievement*
  (audios / workbook)

To order call: 1-800-542-4252